Dear Parent:
Your child's love of reading starts here!

Every child learns to read in a different way and at his or her own speed. Some go back and forth between reading levels and read favorite books again and again. Others read through each level in order. You can help your young reader improve and become more confident by encouraging his or her own interests and abilities. From books your child reads with you to the first books he or she reads alone, there are I Can Read Books for every stage of reading:

SHARED READING
Basic language, word repetition, and whimsical illustrations, ideal for sharing with your emergent reader

BEGINNING READING
Short sentences, familiar words, and simple concepts for children eager to read on their own

READING WITH HELP
Engaging stories, longer sentences, and language play for developing readers

READING ALONE
Complex plots, challenging vocabulary, and high-interest topics for the independent reader

ADVANCED READING
Short paragraphs, chapters, and exciting themes for the perfect bridge to chapter books

I Can Read Books have introduced children to the joy of reading since 1957. Featuring award-winning authors and illustrators and a fabulous cast of beloved characters, I Can Read Books set the standard for beginning readers.

A lifetime of discovery begins with the magical words **"I Can Read!"**

Visit www.icanread.com for information
on enriching your child's reading experience.

To Emma
—D.G.

To Lisa. My inspiration.
—J.P.

*The author gratefully acknowledges the editorial
contributions of Lori Houran.*

I Can Read Book® is a trademark of HarperCollins Publishers.

My Weird School: Talent Show Mix-Up. Text copyright © 2016 by Dan Gutman. Illustrations copyright © 2016 by Jim Paillot. All rights reserved. Manufactured in China. No part of this book may be used or reproduced in any manner whatsoever without written permission except in the case of brief quotations embodied in critical articles and reviews. For information address HarperCollins Children's Books, a division of HarperCollins Publishers, 195 Broadway, New York, NY 10007.
www.icanread.com

ISBN 978-0-06-236743-3 (pbk. bdg.)—ISBN 978-0-06-236740-2 (hardcover)

16 17 18 19 20 SCP 10 9 8 7 6 5 4 3 2 1 ❖ First Edition

I Can Read!™

READING 2 WITH HELP

My WeiRd SchooL

Talent Show Mix-Up

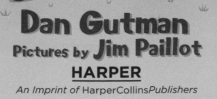

Dan Gutman
Pictures by Jim Paillot

HARPER
An Imprint of HarperCollinsPublishers

My name is A.J. and I hate school.

Monday was the worst.

First my teacher, Mr. Cooper,

passed out some papers.

"Exam time!" he said.

"Exam?" I said.

"I just went to the doctor!"

Everyone laughed,

even though I didn't say anything funny.

5

"He means the *test* kind of exam,"
said know-it-all Andrea.
"Not the doctor kind. Duh!"
So we took a dumb math test.

Then Mr. Cooper said,

"Tomorrow will be much more fun.

It's our class talent show!"

Talent show? Ugh.

I'd rather have an exam.

The test kind OR the doctor kind!

At recess, Andrea acted all worried.

"I have too many talents," she said.

"Should I sing at the show?

Or dance? Or play the flute?"

"How about you sing solo," I said.

"*So low* we can't hear you!"

"Oh, snap!" said my friend Ryan.

Andrea crossed her arms.

"What are YOU going to do?"

"Me?" I said.

"Um, I have too many talents too.

But I'll pick one by tomorrow."

I sat down that night

to make a list of my talents.

1. Dirt bike tricks

2. Peewee football

3. Video games

4. Picking my nose

Then I narrowed it down to

talents I could do at school.

Bummer in the summer!

"Did you pick your talent?"

Andrea asked me the next day.

"Did you pick your nose?" I said.

"You should pick again."

"Oh, snap!" said Ryan.

I wish insulting Andrea was a talent!

Andrea put her name first

on the sign-up sheet for the show.

I put mine last.

I was sure to come up with a talent

before the show ended.

TALENT
SHOW
Andrea
Emily
Neil
Tammy
ALEXIA
Lisa
MICHAEL
A.J.

A+

LUNCH

"Let's get started," said Mr. Cooper.

"Break a leg, Andrea!"

WHAT?!

"Why would you want her to break her leg? That would hurt."

Everybody laughed, even though I didn't say anything funny.

"It's show-biz talk for *good luck*," Mr. Cooper said.

Oh. What's show-biz talk for *I hope an army of ants invades your underwear*?

Andrea's act was lame.
She sang AND danced
AND played the flute.
What a snoozefest!

Then Andrea's crybaby friend
Emily twirled a baton.
It hit her on the head.
She cried and had to go
to the nurse's office.

The talent show went on
for a million hundred hours.
Michael was next to last.
He armpit farted "Yankee Doodle."

"Gross!" said all the girls but Alexia.

"Cool!" said all the boys plus Alexia.

It WAS cool.

But I couldn't even enjoy it.

Because my turn was next.

What was I going to do?!

"Ready, A.J.?" said Mr. Cooper.

I walked to the front of the room.

Everybody was looking at me.

I thought my head was going to explode.

"I don't have a talent!"

I blurted out.

"I'm in the gifted and talented class,

but I guess I'm just gifted.

I do get a lot of presents.

Especially on my birthday."

Everybody laughed,
even though I didn't say
anything funny.

Mr. Cooper laughed the loudest.

"What a great idea to do stand-up for your talent!" Mr. Cooper said.

Huh?

"Standing up is a talent?" I said. Everybody laughed again, even though I STILL didn't say anything funny.

"He means stand-up comedy,"
said Andrea.

"Like telling jokes. Duh!"

Hold on.

"Telling *jokes* is a talent?" I said.

"What else is a talent

I don't know about?

Sleeping? Watching TV?"

I looked at Mr. Cooper.

"Teaching?"

"HA HA HA!"

Mr. Cooper laughed so hard he cried.
Why do people cry when they laugh?
And why don't they laugh when they
cry?

So I had a talent after all.

I was a joke-cracking genius!

"Hey everybody," I said.

"What do you get when you

cross a fish with an elephant?

Swimming trunks!

Get it? *Swimming trunks*?"

Nobody laughed, even though

I DID say something funny.

Comedy is weird.

Just then the bell rang.

"Great job, everyone!"

called Mr. Cooper.

Maybe someday I'll make
people laugh on purpose.
Maybe I'll stand up for a living.
Maybe I'll find out what other
dumb secret talents I have.

But it won't be easy!